The Ugly Duckling

CAREFULLY

Hans Christian Andersen

Nicola O'Byrne

with words by Nick Bromley

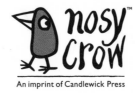

nosy crow

An imprint of Candlewick Press

Once upon a time, there was a mother duck with three pretty ducklings and one—

Wait a minute!

What's that?

I'm trying to read you the story "The Ugly Duckling," but there's something in this book that shouldn't be here!

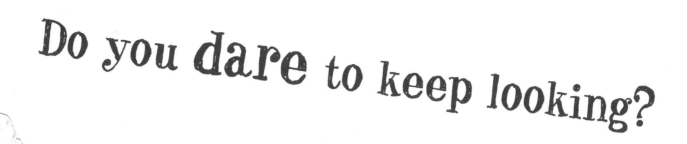

Do you **dare** to keep looking?

You do?

Then turn
the page
very,
very
carefully....

It's a . . .

CROCODILE!

A really big scary one!

What's he doing in
this book?

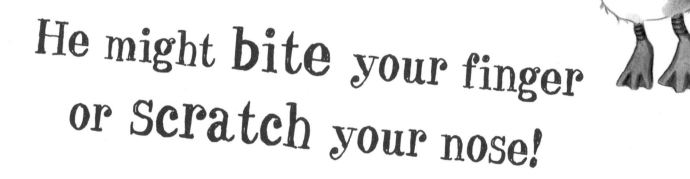

He might **bite** your finger
or **scratch** your nose!

Crocodiles like to do
that.
Stay back
just in case. . . .

Watch out!

He's on the move.

What is he doing?

He's eating the letters!

He must be hungry!

I think his favorite letters to eat are O and S.

St p!

Mr. Cr c dile!

Y u can't eat the letter !

Now he's gobbling up . . .

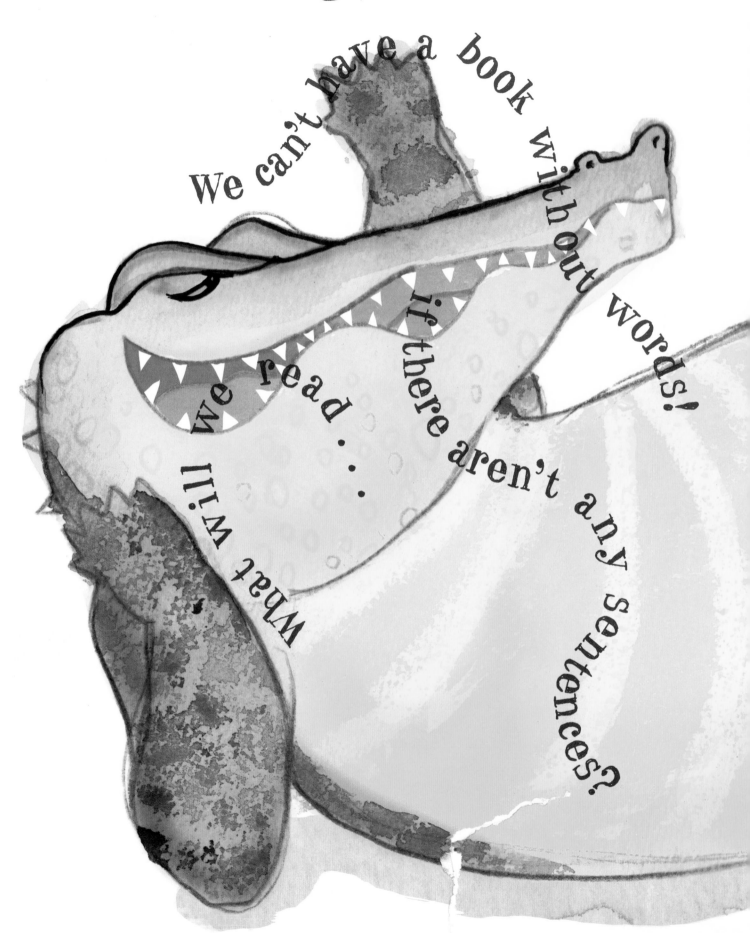

We can't have a book without words!

if there aren't any sentences?

we read . . .

What will

We can't have a book without words!

whole words
and
SENTENCES!

We've got to make him stop.....

Let's try
rocking
the book from

side

to

 side.

That's it. . . . .

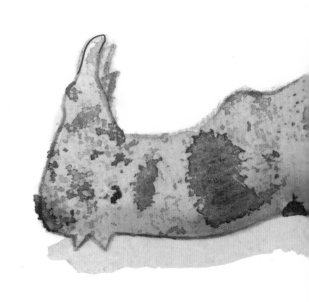

A A A H H . . .
He's sleeping like a baby.
Now . . .

let's find a crayon. If you're going to eat our words, then we're going to draw on you! Mr. Crocodile,

SHHHHH...

He's not such a scary

crocodile now!

Maybe he **is** a
scary crocodile after all!
All that drawing has
woken him up!

And he's not looking too happy
about that tutu.
Crocodiles **don't do ballet!**

Watch out!

It looks as if he's
had enough of
this book.

He's going to
make a run
for it!

Here
he
goes. . . .

Ouch!

Oops! Maybe it isn't so
easy to escape
from a book!

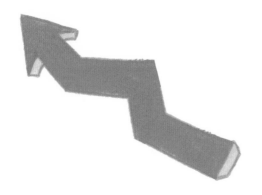

Maybe if you **Shake** the book, he'll fall out.

Hmm. That didn't work.
But look!

He's figured out
what to do.